UNLIKELY WOMEN

Licentiousness, scandals and love

Novella

Anna Maillard-Lamy

Wherever woman is considered, man is free and virtuous.

This novel was first published in French: femmes improbables, libertinage, scandales et amour.

1.

There was a time when I hardly knew what loneliness meant. A time when I vowed to annoy all men and deny myself none of them! They say that marriage is the tomb of love. Yes, that is true, if we considered it only in relation to the sensual delights of the classic couple: the violence of the senses appeases, the ardor of physical need diminishes. But Thomas and I had another vision: to indulge in forbidden curiosities. After the first period of the nuptial union, such a fleeting season, during which life was only tenderness and intoxication, we decided to abandon ourselves with too much ardor to the pleasures of voluptuousness. And since we still couldn't tame this passion, we decided to attack it head on, that is to say, to rejoice in it to excess and make it unbridled. Because, from the beginning, it was obvious that the best way to calm it down was to satisfy it; Sweet complicity and torrential lovemaking followed. Under the influence of our preoccupations, strange plans had been plotted. We have gone to the extreme frontier which separates reason from madness. We didn't talk about it much in our rare moments of solitude; we preferred to guess than to hear, our imagination liked to wander in the shade. To merge into a harmonic whole, our souls had to be transformed, habits, inclinations had to be either developed, or restricted, or destroyed. With or without reflection, we did not see in pleasure only an element of happiness, we linked it closely to the honesty of life, and we only considered it harmful when the calm of the soul could be disturbed by it. Our souls! Wholesomely passionate! The more the soul is chaste, the more easily passion seizes it, and often it burns there with a devouring fire. We had set ourselves limits and then we surpassed them tremendously! For example, never do anything in a quick or superficial way, because you never get anything good in a rush! And yet, we sometimes did things in a quick, superficial way, and that was good! Sometimes, we are only wrong when we think too much! Above all, it was not a debauchery where the excess of pleasure prevented one from enjoying it. We weren't looking for perfection in this universe where people are more pleased by pleasant faults than by essential qualities. Some wanted to do like us, but only imitated from us what is too easily imitable, and they reproduced it without clarity, without style, without life. The imitators are in a way the undertakers of art! Yes, we were artists. All we had to do to be natural was to try to be. They thought they were on solid ground, and took a path from which they could not yet recognize the dark detours. There is a very beautiful word in Plato: "It is with the whole soul that one must go to the truth". I would say that it is with the whole soul that one must go to passion. Because it is constantly burning, somewhere, and if one does what is necessary to go to it, it does not flee from an eternal flight. And once grasped, it stands naked like the truth and shows itself everywhere, around us, sharp, tangible, true, and for this reason is self-sufficient. The libertine is an honest man, and honesty often ends up overcoming adversity, whatever detours one takes to delay the triumph. Thomas is a free man and the one who is too free seems a tyrant and we hate him. Because he spares nothing, we believe him to be full of pride, and that he spares himself; and because he is bitter, he is said to be wicked. But all that was almost in another life. Habits are stronger than principles, more obstinate than passions, and the taste for isolation is ultimately not an eccentricity. I live in a clarity that intoxicates and shines.

It's late June and the sun still smells of winter. Here, I am far from everything. I speak aloud and receive only the echo of my ramblings. It is true to say that the voice is to the heart what echoes are to Nature; it half and weakly renders the language of the eyes. Mine, I don't really know what they look like anymore. But my sight is intact and I revel in it to witness this horizon which reveals itself to be bluish and free. If I could reach it, I would grab it hand and kiss it religiously. I no longer accept seeing others come and contemplate it by my side. It is as if they were defiling its purity and stealing something of my property. And my madness, if it is one, would push me to avoid them like the plague. One day it will speak to me I believe. I feel that it is already beginning to untie the mask of indifference that it willingly puts on. And since there was a time when I found it sad, the show will look like a pretty precocious widow taking off her mourning dress.

Today, if no one comes, it's because I've become mean, I think. If no one invites me now, it's because they consider me a boring old shrew who can only be tolerated at home. Even if I remain a very desirable mother, carrying with infinite grace an attractive slight plumpness; making of my voluminous fair hair and of a charming hue, the most skilful party, with a body still capable of corrupting the most honest judges and the most sincere devotees, at last, I believe it. I have known more beautiful women, who would oblige me to pluck feathers from the angels of a just god and dip them in the azure of the sky to write the words that would describe their charms. And yet, they had less success, more misfortunes and lovers who were only simpletons, who only knew how to languish, what to do with alas!

The last time I saw someone here, I shunned him for some stupidity. In fact, I'm very bored of myself. I should have hurled hurtful insults at him. I am neither crazy nor mean. And I will not give any definition. Neither madness nor malice. It would take me a long time. Then, when we dwell too long on all the terms, we end up no longer agreeing on anything, even when we are, if we leave the surface of things, of the same opinion. Here is a sentence that I cannot like. Long and complex. I don't want to speak well! I want to be deep and clear. Think like Blaise Pascal and talk like a football player. I like football. One of the misfortunes of my life is that people think I'm mocking. Often, it happened to me to say simple things, the others saw it as a joke and thought they were the subject. One day, a man allowed himself, with his status as an only son, to collect my hen's eggs. My one and only hen. I don't remember what happened next. To be honest, it's been a long time since I decided to only remember what suits me. There for example, on my left, if I walk for three minutes, I will come across my husband's house. I know he lives there but I prefer to remember that he has become almost deaf. There's no point in visiting him. I couldn't tire him with my chatter. The last time I saw him he seemed very firm in his resolution to be alone. I respect his choice. He is all friendly. He is still in good shape, but one day he will fall aside and will not be able to get up again; his soul will have gone to rejoin his reason. I talk and I think at the same time. Some sentences catch me. I want to think like Blaise Pascal and talk like a chambermaid! I have nothing against maids or women for that matter. I should have opted for this version from the beginning. My name is Celine. I am 47 years old. Thomas, my husband is in his seventies. Our only son is 26 years old. He hates the companion but continues to visit us once in a blue time.

I don't want to see anyone anymore, I don't want to hear anyone anymore... is it really true that I don't want to anymore? Isn't it just because I don't see anything coming to me that's looking for me!

Tonight Léon and a friend of his will spend the night here, maybe all week. I will go to bed in the other house, and I will begin by telling my husband quite frankly the purpose of my visit.

- Léon will be there tonight, accompanied by his friend, I do not know if they are a couple but I prefer to sleep here and leave them the other house to them.

Lying on the sofa. No gesture. He stares at me oddly, as usual. I approach him to repeat what I just said, in a shrill tone. Barely finished, he squeezes my hand convulsively and slips it under his pants. His large eye, limpid and gentle, seeks my gaze. Embarrassed, but excited, I take off my panties and sit down so that my left foot touches the ground, and my right foot is stretched out, touching his face following the nonchalant movement of his head. I feel his penis. It activates to slip one, then two fingers inside my vagina.

He was tired and his body almost stained with dust. He still continues to cook by himself when none of the maids comes to take care of him. The nearest village is 10 kilometers away and sometimes they are not able to move. He likes it here, Thomas. He had a double goal in getting away from Paris, he wanted to escape a world that reminded him of disastrous memories, and to keep me away from men of my age. After so many years of licentiousness. I'm not complaining here. I like calm. I like the horizon. Me, who grew up in a small apartment that overlooked an ugly building.

It's almost midnight. I didn't like Léon's girlfriend, Jade, too quiet. The four of us dined together. In silence so as not to disturb Thomas. But at dessert time, he was already gone, and we still hesitate to talk. Léon and Jade were seated at the table, very far from each other but their eyes were looking for each other. The evening passed fairly quietly; I was surprised, knowing Léon's impetuous mood. Jade ate a little and flew away like a bird after circling the table, giving us all a kiss on the forehead with a certain little lip sound, which is usually the echo of pleasure. A tall brunette dressed in white, whose profile has so much grace: woman to the tips of her nails! Confident. Léon is rather a small man constantly tormented by the fear that he will not be taken seriously, that he will not be counted for something; speaking loudly to force the attention that one might not otherwise give to his words. Mistaking pride for greatness, making noise while walking, opening and closing doors violently, always frowning to look terrible, talking only about his former female conquests and his football career if he had not suffered a cruciate ligament injury at the age of 15. His motto: "I am small, but terrible" and still thinks he hasn't received enough.

The air is unbreathable in this small room. I want to go out for a walk and smell some fresh air, but I'm afraid they'll suspect me of spying on them if they see me.

– Since you're not sleeping, let's talk, Jade asks me, coming to sit on a chair to my right in the garden, no sound detected her walking, she glided silently on the grass.

– Which of you two is having the most fun?" I ask her.

She affectionately takes my hand, which I do not seek to withdraw. I purse my lips and become more attentive.

– We've been together for three months. We get along well. He never seems to be bothered by the ten-year age gap, I believe he loves me, and I cherish him like a virtuous mother fondly cherishes, the least beautiful, the most stupid, the most to be pitied of his children!

I go stiff for a few seconds, nod and shake her hand nervously. This detail should normally be taken as direct outrage, but it reasons differently from her mouth. She lowers her eyes a little before continuing:

– May God come to my aid and not punish me for loving him like this!" tell me, Léon hardly ever mentions you, tell me a little about you two, Thomas and you.

– First of all, what is called faith is something that is completely foreign to me, otherwise I was in the middle of a journey, without friends, without support, almost without money, and my path crossed that of Thomas, I launched after a long sigh before continuing, I had a body full of freshness and chaste poetry. I wanted to please him, and I did, it was a pretty weird situation, but each step made the next one inevitable. At first he was surprised to find me so well informed about everything, then he began to find me too talkative.

She sketches a smile, I continue:

– Thomas was the passion that made me happy, whose first sweetness is still present in my mind, and whose memory will always be dear to me. Some chapters of our life will forever remain a wonderful memory, and there are memories that are enough for a lifetime.

Without departing from her calm but still with a hesitant look, she said to me:

– First, I believe firmly without asking myself why I believe. If someone asks, I will not be embarrassed to provide my reasons. But this is for others, not for me. You know what, today, in this solitary and empty place, you are bored, I think you need spectators, to magnificently display all your beauties that Providence often scatters among many.

Her voice shakes her being and charms my spirit! We look at each other, there is a strange silence. A most bizarre impression. When she speaks, everything seems to be silent to listen to her.

- Léon told me that you were mean, especially with women, why are being nice to me? she asks me.

– I'm not as bad as the legend claims, it's just that I'm more and more often very bored with myself...

She interrupts me by gently withdrawing her hand:

– It's just that you've become a bitter enemy of any scandal of which you can no longer be the heroine.

– I salute your audacity.

– I thank you.

– You are another me!

– Oh good ! To help you judge better, I will paint my picture, I slip everywhere, I force the doors that are the best closed and it seems to me that I possess the terrible gift of ubiquity, and, like a ghost from the old legends, I appear , I obsess and terrify.

– There's a grain of truth in the old legends, but you know, you can't accomplish with a certain conscience what you want by pure calculation.

– No doubt, but nice subterfuge so that you don't talk about yourself more, I understand, it is very difficult to talk about yourself: you risk making yourself unbearable.

I quickly realize that she has just swindled me with remarks that I did not want to make. Especially not so quickly. There is triumph in her sly smile. But I admit it to myself, the conversation seems to be taking such a pleasant turn. You must always be wary of the words of such a woman. They are surprising, like the boxes, quiet in appearance, from which suddenly emerges, when they are opened, a disheveled devil. We never predict how they will end. A short proposition, a single word, suddenly added, changes their whole meaning, or gives them an intention that they did not seem to have. One does not converse with Jade as with the others.

My husband makes noise while peeing. Fatigue warns us that we have sufficiently satisfied our curiosity for today. She gets up, places a kiss on my temple and leaves. I go back to my bed and stare at the ceiling of my room, which only a weak ray of the moon illuminates. Not one attacks a woman without having made what is called a plan, without having spent a night walking around and turning the position around like an author who ties up his plot in his head. She does theatre. That's the only thing she said at dinner. She must have googled my name and found the only article available online where the author referred to me as the rising star of the theatre. It was in another life. Jade is among that band of women who make seduction the goal of their thoughts and the great business of their lives. She looks like me. A strange feeling of helplessness and unreality overtakes me.

I slept like a baby. It's almost ten o'clock and I still have trouble getting up. The weather is nice. I wash my face and take my time to make myself beautiful, without knowing why. Hesitatingly, I head for my house.

—Hello, Jade throws me with the smile of a woman to whom we have never been able to say no.

– Hello, I reply.

Dressed in extreme elegance, she is busy cleaning the furniture. I take my coffee without saying a word. Going up the stairs to take a shower, she said to me:

– In fact, Léon and Thomas went for a hike and they plan to come back late.

–Okay, I told her with an air of indifference.

This may be my fastest shower of my life. Coming out of the bath, without panties and without a bra, my hair almost still wet, I go down to lie down on a sofa in the living room. Jade is talking on the phone, in the garden. Last night, it seems to me that she combined the coolness of the hunter with the glance of a pirate to attack me, she chased me, pushed me, beat me from sentence to sentence, from word to word, flushed me out from defense to defense, dully narrowed the circle of the attack, pressed me, cornered me, forced me and finally held me, at the end of the conversation , in her hand, me, throbbing, heart pounding, out of breath like a bird caught on the run! She applies brilliantly this maxim of Aristotle: say only what's necessary, and say it right.

She sits on the sofa, on the side of my feet. She fixes me with a penetrating gaze, and after a long moment of hesitation, she asks me, in a woman's voice that descends to the last recess of her heart:

– Isn't it a principle repeated everywhere, a fact affirmed, that it is enough to tell a woman three times that she is pretty, for her to thank you the first time, for her to believe you at the second one, and so that at the third she will reward you?

Her words plunge me into a vague reverie. Praise is a weapon, with what skill, she uses it! Struck with a stupor that freezes the words on my lips, it takes me forever to pull myself together, to realize that in order to flatter people shout very loudly what they don't mean; the simple trickle of water becomes a great river. I answer her :

– I am touched by the good opinion you have of me and flattered by your compliments. I would like to deserve them.

She is strangely attractive. Taken by a crisis of curiosity, the interest is born and exaggerates disproportionately. Never has a woman appeared to me more beautiful, more desirable. She bends down to kiss my hand, which I brought to my chest earlier. Her body seems to make a promise to my soul, my soul has already made hers for her body. And the heart waits for an almost unknown joy. She has this that I can't describe so sweet and so powerful that disarms. She is very close to my throat, she forgets herself, she gets carried away, she tumbles on the big sofa conducive to embraces, her hand wanders off, and we find ourselves a few seconds later, without us really know how it happened, both naked. Only the first step counts and it's been taken!

Jade has no consideration for age or rank, she respects neither youth nor position; she wants, she takes. It seems to me that she would be almost ashamed not to flaunt her vice. This little drawing-room never has too much daylight; the light arrives there through clouds of various colors, and to lull her body favorable to the abandonment of coquetry, it descends laden with skilfully calculated shades.

Lying on top of me now, she deliciously bites my ear before whispering:

– I confess that I feel devoured by a need always resurgent and never satisfied, you hear me, rascal, this day must be marked by some adventure that we do not read about in novels.

Eyes half closed, my right hand ventures to caress her back.

– Last night, she was about to launch before I interrupted her:

– If one cannot always tear oneself away from the boredom of the first, one always has at least the second to compensate oneself.

I take her hand, I kiss it; she takes mine, she squeezes it; a clasping hand wants something; I give her a kiss with all my heart, and redouble several times in favor of a beautiful mouth that always offers itself as I pass. My ardor increases, its fire is communicated to mine; our eyes already, fixed on each other.

—I'm like you, I find the evening boring, the night long, we really have fun only in the morning, she said.

—You animated a marble, fear that it reproaches you one day, to have taken it out of its peaceful insensitivity, I told her in a tone of confidence.

She smiles, shyly.

—Weigh my words, they are engraved in your heart to never be erased, I ordered her.

— I want you, but I fear the consequences of a passion which I feel that I will do my only business, she said before rubbing her crotch against mine.

Now holding her face in my hands, I tell her:

—You disturb all my projects, you destroy the plan for the rest of my life, a host of ideas embarrass and afflict me. My reason rejects all my wishes, combats all my desires and rises up against all my feelings.

She smiled, a voluptuous smile accompanied by such a burning gaze.

— I will be as discreet as my shadow, she says in a tone that convinces.

What must be done, we have to do it frankly and cheerfully, isn't it true? The pleasure hides the shame. I reverse her suddenly and get busy licking her clitoris, sucking her in a little, pressing her breasts. Her first moans are heard, and her legs, which she knows how to get a thousand benefits, convulse. Her screams are getting louder and louder. She grabs my hand to lick my fingers ; I return to her with vivacity; she takes me where I'm sure I go very willingly. Nothing is like a woman who has a temper, and who has been frustrated in her expectation. It is no longer taste, it is passion; it is no longer desire, it is fury; I don't believe that there is anything in the world more vivid than the possession of an object of this kind: I attack a place that is offered to me; I slip two fingers into the depths, I extend my conquests in an atmosphere whose entrances had been made easy for me. I go back a bit, and my mouth now begins to devour her tits so appetizing. Jade's body looks like a beautiful promise, she knows it and she thinks she's a beautiful song. The spirit of the times besieges her, it awakens her senses at all hours.

Our antics lasted forever. We took a shower together and then she decided to dress me as she pleased. A short skirt and a pretty tight top. We were as calm as if nothing had happened to us. I explained to her that I had to spend the rest of the day in Thomas's hovel, and accompanied me to the door. Before depositing a last kiss, she said to me:

– If you wonder why I dared, know that one has no weakness, without others noticing it, passion is painted in the eyes; look at mine, aren't they the mirror of innocence?

These were her last words. She will leave tomorrow with Léon. They return to Paris to closely follow the making of a film that Léon has decided to finance. He bought the favors of a great director who promised him in exchange to assign an important role to Jade. He wants to make her a movie star.

As soon as I was lying on my bed, I was gripped by the kind of grief one feels when one has lost something very dear, and one really wants to conceal how sensitive one is to this loss. I add to the regret of losing a happiness, the shame of having tasted it. I give myself wrongs to diminish hers. I want to call her and insult her, but it's very criminal when you've angered those you wanted. In addition, Jade resembles me: one was born to love, to sing, to laugh, to deceive, to return to one's love like the swallow to its nest, like the wave in the hollow of the rock on the beach; born to bring delight and despair to the partner, we know by heart what can thrill a woman's sensitivities, captivate her interest, bring about a softening or nervousness in her, touch the most delicate fibers of her being.

2.

Two weeks have passed without bringing any important events. I continue to take care of my very pretty hen. I regain a taste for my loneliness, even if the place looks more and more like a foreign country to me.

Thomas, always in his corner, takes advantage of each of my visits to fuck me as if I didn't belong to him, as if he was almost ashamed to still need that at his age. I read a quote written by a woman, and I don't know how exact the thing is: "Love, which is only an episode in the life of a man, is the whole story of life of a woman". Why mention this? I do not know ! Yesterday, he was terribly annoyed, his nerves were tense like the strings of a violin, his expression morose, his bearing bent, in an intense dejection . I want to talk to him at length, or start writing him letters, but there are things that are useless to say, because of the difficulty of proving that one really means them. Sometimes I don't recognize him anymore. It was with an inexpressible appetite that he enjoyed watching others see me, touch me, kiss me. And when the happy guest came out of my intimacy with his softened penis, he threw himself on it, sucking it like a professional prostitute, and only planting the device deep inside me when it was as hard as a metal bar. And sometimes he was not shy about putting the dick inside him, a dick still wet from the wetness of my vagina.

He loved me in his own way, with the ardor of a healthy passionate soul. It was never vulgar, it was a passion like no nobler. Always by my side, at home or in a hotel room, or elsewhere, he scrutinized my soul, while another, or several, made my body their business. I saw judges and lawyers, high army officers and their wives, ministers and their mistresses, some pretty, some famous. For years, drowned in an ocean of delights, I got drunk on forbidden curiosities, and everything I touched, everything I encountered or saw, brought weakness to my will, trouble to my imagination and softening. On all sides arose temptation around me, not only the gross and material temptation, but also that affecting the peace of my senses, irritating the appetites of my fancy and the curiosities of my caprice. But the course of so much Parisian prosperity was suddenly stopped when Thomas gave up his political career, barely launched, almost at the moment when all his hopes were exalted and became certainties, after a dispute within the party about his candidacy for mayor of Paris. Quarrel of ambition! He saw passing on his left people whom he had known for a long time on his right. He talked to them a lot and he was disappointed. He then sold all his shares, interned Léon in a high school and brought me here. What precious anecdotes, if I abandoned myself to the drift of my memories. My day started at the times when we go out together, at the times when we receive; those which precede were only a wait, generally spent in bed, not however an idle wait, since my habit was to read, think, write down my thoughts in bed.

Jade haunts my thoughts. She has the art of pleasing me. Her scent follows me. Like a sweet smell that still follows you long after you have left it. I miss her warm body, too. Her picture. The most tender, fiery woman, throwing herself into my arms and devouring me with kisses; my body still feels its burning hugs. My attraction to her body turns to obsession. Fueled also by the attitude she adopted once the effect of the orgasm disappeared. Her face, so happy that it seemed to me that I had never seen such an expression of joy, although she tried to contain it. I look forward to our next meeting. I may even go to see her without warning. I experience a kind of intoxication that poetry alone can convey. Reality catches up with me, and reminds me that I am a woman who has already learned that joy is fleeting, playful, airy, intermittent and wants to be fleeting. The grief is serious, deep, inescapable. The lack is heavy, monotonous, obstinate, it sinks into the sides like a line that remains.

I place a plate that I don't quite know what it was doing in my hand. I raise my skirt and gently rub my pussy with the end of my cooker. I pick up the pace. Thomas enters, embarrassed to witness this scene, especially this way. He turns around abruptly as if caught in the act of indiscretion.

– Come back, I ordered him, come back, I continue in a pleading voice.

He manages to conceal his confusion and walks towards me, releases my hidden nipple. No time for foreplay. He undresses very quickly. I take off my clothes. I bite his lips. The desire is far too all-consuming to dwell on anything else. His penis is already hard, I've known better but his erection is more than enough. Just seeing his cock in this state makes my whole body tense. I feel his excitement growing. He avoids seeing me in the eye, and tries to slide his organ into me, standing up. We quickly realize that we have never enjoyed quickly with this position. We move quickly to the next room. We lie down on a large bed for the guests to give free rein to our devouring desire. He doesn't waste his time, he thrusts his cock inside me. Fiercely. Ferociously. Miraculously, my vagina is still quite tight. "Go ahead my darling". The comings and goings go beyond my pussy. It's like discovering a new dimension. My state is hypnotic. I'm salivating. I go into a long, loud distortion. He continues his back and forth, and his hands are busy squeezing my breasts. He tries to hold me back. But I no longer control my body. My convulsions get the better of him and his sperm spreads over my leg. He fingers me. I beg him to let me breathe for a moment. I regain my strength and offer him perhaps the best blowjob of his life.

Barely out of my shower, I receive a message from Jade: "Hello Céline, Léon and I immediately thought of you when an actress informed us of her impossibility to reach the filming location. Everyone is nice here. It's a small role, which wouldn't require much effort from you. Come baby, come give a night of perfect happiness to the one that your refusal would stab. Please answer me without delay ". It's Jade! Who speaks of happiness; this shore where all the tumult of our appetites comes to die! She is a sincere woman. A wrong feeling never sounds right. My pulse is pounding, my blood is burning, and my chest is tight. Tomorrow, whether it's windy, whether it's raining or whether the sun dissolves the bitumen, I'll go to Paris. I will go on foot if necessary, even if I am able to find a great number of reasons to avoid such a task.

After three hours of driving in my car, I arrive in Paris! The serious sky is a loveless blue! I go to the hotel, happy as youths in good fortune who leave light-footed, their hearts beating with holy emotion, worried only to know whether the mistress they will conquer will be blond or dark-haired. It's almost noon, in an hour Jade will pick me up. She sent me yesterday the text to learn by heart. I memorized it in no time. My scenes will be shot mainly this afternoon in an apartment, then in an alley somewhere in Paris.

Lying on the bed. The door opens abruptly. It's Jade, she quickly closes the door behind her and drags on, standing, staring at me with a slight smile. After a long minute of mute contemplation, during which I stare at her with more joy than a lover hugging his long-awaited lover. Her easy successes increased her audacity. Guessing me already ready for any event, for all possibilities, she widens her eyes, throws her bag, undresses completely and gives me the view of all her beauties. Jade, naked, is the most beautiful sight on which the eye can rest. I calm my emotion. With a deliberate step, she walks over to the bed, throws herself on top of me, and in a sugary voice, she lets me know that we don't have much time. I find in the charm of this visit, all the fires that I thought I had dampened. "Let yourself admire the treasures I possess, take some ideas of the possible perfection of a mortal being." she seems to be saying. She turns me over on the bed and crosses my arms behind my back as if to handcuff me. The position is uncomfortable but I'm dying to feel her skin against mine. Pain alone gives pleasure all its reality, makes it emerge from the depths of the soul, illuminates it, clarifies it by contrast, as a cloud reveals to us the limpidity of the air, a ripple of the sea, the azure continuous flow. Quickly, she takes off my jeans, slips her hand under my shirt to squeeze my breast, and pushes two fingers with the other hand, without removing my panties, deep in my pussy. She leaves my breast to grab my chin. The temple glued to the bed, the deformed mouth, it penetrates two fingers that I start to suck. She slides those same two fingers inside her. I take a deep breath and close my eyes for a moment. She goes down my panties to the feet. I hardly dare admit it to myself, but I'm just waiting for one thing: his mouth sucking my clitoris. The vulva very wet, the thighs wide open. In contact with her lips with my swollen vagina, I swallowed my saliva, opening my eyes wide. Jade is a goddess! I comply with her wishes! I try to grab her hair to encourage her to stay in this position. Her mouth is greedy, and when she tries to introduce a finger into my ass, an electric wave runs through my whole body. My orgasmic convulsions pushes her back a little in a somewhat abrupt gesture. She turns around, we rub sex. Sometimes tenderly, sometimes fiercely. Our hands cross our bodies mutually.

– You were bored without respite, and it was pity to see moping such a beautiful creature, she says confusedly just before she throws herself aside.

– Let's go ?!

I immerse myself in the contemplation of her gray eyes that her dark eyelashes make at times seem almost black. I go back over the years, I am again young, lively and cheerful.

- Let's go ! I answer her after a long moment.

After half an hour of road and silence, we arrive at the building where the filming is taking place at this very moment. We go up the stairs, the first door on the right is open, Jade asks me to stay there and walks along the corridor to look for the director. A canvas, hanging on the wall just at the entrance, fascinates me. I contemplate the painting for a long time without being able to know if it's a sunset or a sunrise. Jade returns, accompanied by Patrick, the director. His face has an expression of singular indulgence, mingled with vain pride. He takes himself for a philosopher too, he who is only a vulgar public entertainer. I've seen him on TV before. But I didn't come to my age without meeting enough people I had seen on TV before. And no one was up to the image he wanted us to keep of him. After the hugs, still smiling, holding on a leash the hungry pack of the most ardent desires, I feel that darling hand gently pressing mine. He is an ordinary man. After a short friendly chat, I confirm myself in my assessment, I do not find him interesting. And to tell the truth, he strikes me as tiring, brooding, and common-looking. We discuss the scenes, the features that I have to let appear. From my walk, my look and my voice.

A young woman approaches.

– This is my girlfriend, he said proudly.

Why is this beautiful young girl hanging on the arm of this monster?

Immense role of chance or pure calculations!

There are enough people but I'm not in the mood to start a conversation. I don't know them well, and to a certain extent I take care to know who Orestes is and who Agamemnon is to avoid speaking lightly, in front of them, either of Clytemnestra or Iphigenia. A cameraman arrives with a smug laugh, and staring at me, he searches in my face a chatty expression. With a calm face, I assume an evasive air and make him understand that I need to stay focused to interpret my role as it should.

Léon arrives and introduces me to the actor who will play the role. My passage is very simple. And I didn't even ask for the whole script. I am a client who arrives at the office of a young lawyer. We discover that we were neighbors in the distant past, that we had a one night stand. I leave his office despite all his attempts. He follows me running and in an alley, we talk a bit, we shake hands, and that's the end of my passage. I understand that the rest of the film, the lawyer will spend his time explaining himself to his wife. A bad movie!

I let my eyes wander in the room, azure stained glass windows let the day filter through an ecclesiastical decor. I converse a bit with the actor. Rather handsome man. Nice. But I can't read his eyes, and whatever his feelings, they absolutely escape my observation. Others a little far from us are chatting with vivacity.

In one take, the first scene is a success and everyone applauds me. Patrick asks Jade and Léon to go to the studio to record the voice for certain scenes. Léon shrugged his shoulders at first, but faced with the haughty, severe director, too aware of his value, Léon made himself small. His life goes on with absorbing work, and absolute inexperience in what is not his business. And his only guides are suspicious, malevolent people, interested in deceiving him. “It wouldn't take us long,” Jade says as if to comfort him, in the tone of a woman accustomed to commanding.

– Relax, everything will be fine, Léon tells me passing next to me without kissing me.

"See you tonight," Jade told me playfully.

Getting in the car with Patrick, he asks the driver to leave us alone for a moment.

– We had to send the actors' documents signed, and Léon didn't think it necessary to bother you with the paperwork and he signed for you. Don't worry, it's not an adult film, but it would be nice if you agreed to add a light kiss to the scene, and most likely, we won't even keep it during editing, it's is just in case the art direction deems…

I interrupt him to say: “Okay”. There is no artistic direction or even a superior, he decides everything.

He jumped as if he was going to take his flight out of the window, and go truly untimely bursts of gaiety. I'm about to imitate him so much I'm surprised by his reaction and his singular figure. He wears a long cap and large glasses behind which shines a most lively look. There is a seduction against which I hardly try a defense, a fascination which I do not know how to escape. Something in me dreamed of this scene.

– Really, madam, you make me happy, said Patrick when the last tremors of his joy had calmed down a little.

We arrive. Patrick orders everyone to follow him and asks the truck driver to park so that no one can access the alley; so that no one can see anything especially. On the other end, it was a very large garden. By the time the two technicians place their equipment, the make-up artist settles the details, an endless discussion between Patrick and the main actor, it's already the start of the night. I can make out the tops of the oaks which are beginning to shake with the cool wind blowing through their foliage, the branches colliding with each other. The muffled screams of the inhabitants are heard in the distance. Paris is the city in Europe which worries the least about hidden suffering. The smell of the place seems to testify against these inhabitants not knowing how to enjoy the hours which flee, nor the people who pass.

There arises in me an apprehension, a slight fear of being disappointed. If I were to repent of having come! Is it without imprudence that I will see my past again, all the magic decoration of my first soul, in this scene when I will put on a show in front of strangers.

Stock ! The actor presses me against the wall, slowly directs his mouth to mine. The two cameramen move around, the sound engineer not far from us, two others from the lighting team too. The makeup artist is sitting on a chair next to Patrick. The atmosphere reminds me of so many memories, my youth, the springtime of my life, the real season when passion was burning with all its fire ; then, impetuous, exalted, fickle and inconstant. I kiss the actor, slip my hand into his pants and pull out his penis. I turn against the wall. He lowers my jeans and pretends to penetrate me. He puts both his hands on my shoulders. He's good, but he doesn't improvise. Each of his gestures was certainly dictated to him by the director, in detail, perhaps by Jade. I feel his penis brush against my pussy well lodged in my panties. A sweet and painful thrill is my youth.

—Perfect! We're going home! Patrick throws us.

I pull myself together and leave the place to take a taxi. A gust of wind, like the brushing of a fan, brings me back to myself completely. My car is in the hotel parking, I'm going home tonight. I walked for five minutes so that no one asked me to drop me off. The decor of Paris makes me nauseous. I suddenly hurry, I pass a young man tying his shoe next to another much older man, both tipsy, lying on the ground. As I passed, a dog yelped as it fled. Birds give a shrill cry and decamp at high speed. Finally a taxi! A man almost begs me to give him my number. Inaccessible to all seduction, deaf to his insinuations, I get into the taxi, but a fleeting smile still lights up my face before closing the door. The driver is an old man, he talks on the phone. I understand that it's his wife, a happy old voice, which one guesses good, escapes from the headphones and answers the clear questions of her husband : what she was preparing for dinner.

Seeing me leaving the hotel after only a few hours, the receptionist asks me if something is wrong, that they could reimburse me if I could show any failure in the service.

"I don't care," I told him.

On the verge of insulting him for nothing, I calm down when I see my car arrive.

To extract myself from this Parisian atmosphere, from the traffic jam and the horns, I try to remember my last appearance on a theater stage, my last reply to a talented actor who played a twenty-year-old lover, begging me to tell him if he was loved "tomorrow you will know", was my answer, tearing myself from his arms. The decor changes, the lights come on, and true to my word, I addressed these pretty verses to the one I was happy to confess for my lover:

My heart sighs at dawn.

During the day, a trifle makes me blush,

In the evening, my heart still sighs,

I feel pain and pleasure.

I dream of you when I sleep.

Your name agitates me, it seizes me.

I think of you when I wake up

Everywhere your image follows me.

When you speak, your touching voice,

In my senses carries the pleasure.

Your appearance disturbs and enchants me.

I am looking for you and would like to flee from you.

Yes, everything in my heart reminds you,

I enjoy my happiness a hundred times over.

Ah! tell me what to call

What's going on in my heart?

These verses resonate with me as if I have just hummed them for the first time.

"I just hit the road. It's not love that touches my heart, no, it's not. It's much better, much more, it's the assembly of all the most tender feelings. If you doubt it, you don't deserve to inspire them. Goodbye, the me that I love more than myself". Voicemailed to Jade, voice shaking. I turn off my phone so I don't have to explain myself.

After the endless zigzags of the road that winds around the mountain, among the fragrant chestnut trees, I finally arrive home, I breathe a peace there, on this enchanting night, with the balmy breezes that come from the great lake of the region. The air seems to me twenty times purer than in Paris. I go slowly, along the slope, almost happy that it is so late, and that no one is waiting for me anymore. I feel free, and nothing disturbs this first feeling of arrival. How sweet the air is to breathe! I notice, from a distance, the lights still on in Thomas' living room. He must still be awake because I can also hear his television; he turns the volume up and he can barely hear. I'm tired but I want to go tell him I'm back. I hesitate. I'll take my shower and then decide.

Coming out of my shower, it rings. He never enters without ringing first. Going down the stairs, I see him, frozen in the doorway. I take him to the middle of the garden. I take off his shorts and suck him off. It does not band. I get up, approach his ear and tell him that I was fucked in an alley in Paris, that strangers saw us. As I spread out the details, his instrument of pleasure took shape. I'm dizzy, on the verge of fainting. I faint.

3.

A month has passed. Almost no news from Jade or Léon. Except some messages on whatsapp, some voice messages too. Her voice numbs the pain, it has the softness of a mountain spring. I indulge in sad reflections. How many things in me obsess me without yet being clearly formulated. I shunned Thomas this morning. There are bad days when you get up you find your slippers inside out, when you cut yourself while waxing, when all the bad things happen to you at once, and when you meet people you love, we are still surly and we treat them very badly. I barely sleep, as soon as I close my eyes, an elf opens them in spite of me. And when I manage to sleep, it's a tiring and restless sleep. I converse with the absent, I hear their voices, I am moved by their smile, I evoke what is no longer, from the peaks of the present, I recapture the past, and I try to reach the future . Age makes you think, reality too, and many illusions dissipate on contact with true unbridled passion. When I sleep, the same image always illuminates my dreams: Jade. She does not react to certain messages. I would love to be with her. And I console myself by telling myself that sometimes when love becomes unbridled, the appetite is lost. If I had the facility of never moving away from her, I would lose the pleasure of wishing for her, of waiting for her, perhaps of pleasing her. We do not think of rejoicing in the presence of a lover when we have her perpetually before our eyes. She knows that I get my rejuvenation from her, and she doesn't want me to give her blessing explicitly: a heart born generous suffers when he is denied the means of showing his gratitude! We've been spending more time together Thomas and I lately. We sometimes talk about the past but he pretends to forget our secrets when I don't want him to remember them. True to himself, he always prays to ask for my happiness, without examining whether it is on him that it must always depend. He let me know a few days ago when I sent him a long text that ends with: "I would forbid myself any happiness that don't not come from you, if one day you decided to keep me for yourself alone, I would refuse any pleasure of which you would not have the joy of feeling yourself the godfather, alone". Sometimes he looks to me like a satiated and bored old man, sometimes he experiences a few perfidious and tempting reminiscences, and still believes himself capable of supporting the losses and the shocks of sensual voluptuousness.

If Jade wasn't Léon's girlfriend, I would have invited her so we could have sex in front of Thomas. I think Léon likes her, but he'll never be in love enough to get over that feeling. I saw him envelope her in a singular gaze, abandoned to her kiss during dinner as to music. But I know him, mistrust is born in him with an almost pathological suddenness. Léon's story is very simple: a seducer who entices a woman, despises this woman for giving in to him, and forgets to despise himself for seducing her. But he remains, most of the time, a man of common sense, somewhat depressed by life. He wants to enjoy, he wants to appear, spread and impose himself. He considers himself as a rare metal, as a happy combination of nature. And he wants to have many children. It seems to him that the more offspring he grows, the more his life will be enlarged, extended.

The film was finally bought by a streaming platform and will be released today. I watched the trailer where one can see me walk into the lawyer office. I'll watch it tonight if I have the courage, or invite Thomas to watch it with me if I don't.

Thomas comes to find me. He is agitated, his eyes are haggard, his voice is troubled, his face is marked by poorly wiped tears. Smartphone in hand.

- Listen darling, it will not happen again and not knowing how you were going to take the thing, I hesitated to tell you about it and it was not even expected that they keep it in the editing.

He doesn't seem to know what I'm talking about! He opens whatsapp, clicks on a link that has just been sent to him. A porn site. A sextape. I quickly recognize the singular room of a second home that we had before Thomas decided to sell everything. The camera is like hanging somewhere on a chandelier. Thomas, much younger, brings a chair. Two black men throw me on the bed! Feet and hands tied! I grab his smartphone and ask him in a feverish voice:

—What is this !

His tongue becomes bitter and pasty, he staggers, I miss breathing. Léon sends me several voice messages. He calls, I hang up. "What is this scene? who the hell gave you the idea to make it. You forced Patrick to add this scene to show everyone what you've always been a whore, did you know him before? That's why you quickly accepted?! Jade knew? Answer. It's Léon!

—I had been blackmailed with this video, I gave up everything to protect you, throws me Thomas.

I catch tears in his eyes.

I don't know where to turn. Thomas is still down there, troubled by fear, spurred on by remorse, oppressed by grief. The idea of filing a complaint was discussed, but why? I had Jade on the phone who explained to me that in just a few hours after the film aired, social networks were flooded, my photos everywhere, the scene shot in the alley was viewed by hundreds of thousands of time, whoever had information about me saw their tweet liked to become a trend on their own. Someone shared the sextape probably with this in mind and it's unclear if there are others. We wait. Jade is on the way and she made me promise not to tell Léon, he's staying in Paris, and when I call him he'd rather insult me than try to talk.

I want to sleep and only wake up when nothing reminds me of this nightmare. Life weighs on me. I pour myself a glass of whiskey. I want to immerse myself in an ecstasy from which it will take me eternity to return.

"Jade!" I said, barely awake. This unexpected appearance interrupts my reverie with a jolt of awakening.

—It's me yes! she said, stroking my shoulder tenderly.

I try to get up but she stops me by suggesting that I should stay in bed.

– Thomas left when he saw me arrive, I'm going to prepare food, shall I call him? she asks me.

– I'll call him when dinner is ready, what time is it already?

– It's time to get drunk, a poet would have said, and it's almost eight o'clock for ordinary mortals!

–You drove here, you must be dead tired.

–I couldn't let you go through this alone.

–Thank you, apparently the pain watched my joys.

– Do not worry, everything ends up working out. Consider yourself lucky, you had at least your moments of glory, my life is a long melodrama, tearful, prosaic, without greatness, filled with small miseries and bland annoyances.

I smile at her. As I stood up, I squeezed her hand a little, saying, “Thank you!”.

—If it matters, Léon and I broke up this morning, she said, closing the door.

4.

Léon is more understanding. I had him on the phone this morning, he was planning to pick us up to file a complaint. I dissuaded him on the pretext that we don't want to spend a second explaining ourselves either in public or in front of the police. Jade slept downstairs on a large comfortable sofa, Thomas had dinner with us last night before returning home. The atmosphere was calm. Serene. Almost cheerful. Jade is more tender than me, more sensitive; she is more sincere in her passion, gives herself up entirely, sacrifices herself without reserve.

– In the morning, I like to get lost on the summit of this little mountain, I say to Jade, who takes her coffee in the garden, to breathe the more subtle and fresher air of the morning: it cleans the brain.

She sets down the cup of coffee, looks at me with a bewitching smile, and says:

– It was on the top of the mountains that the Ancients went to adore the Divinity; it was on Mount Sinai that Moses...

I interrupt her to tell her: "let's go, you will be both my goddess and my religion". Thomas, hesitantly walks towards us. He greets us and asks us if we need anything. I shovel Jade and it seems to me that she is suspending the movement, the circulation, in my chest: everything stops inside me, to hear the noise her lips are making against mine. I catch my breath and ask Thomas to accompany us on this hike which promises to be entertaining. After a quick smile, and without honoring Jade with a single look, he goes back into the living room, leaving behind him bursts of laughter. I follow, and immediately he shakes his head curtly. "You ruminate too much, and that only suits old people reduced to poking by the fireside, I tell him with a tentative smile that seems so cheerful before continuing, they've broken up" and without insisting I go out to sit at the table with Jade, leaving the ball in his court.

We take a shortcut before swerving to the left to enter boldly into a maze of small stony, uneven, rutted, winding paths. The climb is so rough that my legs buckle halfway, my tongue becomes bitter and mushy, Jade holds on. Thomas staggers, on the verge of falling, exhausted, almost determined to turn back, Jade congratulates him at every step.

—We go back if you want, I said.

—The stairs carved into the rock will then facilitate the ascent, he retorts.

My eyes circle the horizon. Sweat beaded on my forehead. Not a living soul. Happy to find a setting familiar to my heart. I know the place like the back of my hand, but next to Jade, I discover it like a stranger. The sight of this spectacle frees us from all fatigue. The three of us undress. Thomas, standing, sees his sex erect perhaps like never before. Jade pulls me down and slips his penis into my mouth. I enjoy taking it out completely, before diving into it at full speed. She has one hand on my head, the other excites Thomas more by massaging his nipples. I want to catch my breath, but she stops me by pressing both my head and Thomas's buttocks. I'm about to puke. In a long cry, Thomas arches his back and enjoys. I recognize the man I agreed to marry well: in these fits of furious ardour, he has a red face, inflamed eyes, burning lips, a frothy, drooling, runny mouth. I'm hot, wet, boiling. He lies down and watches us devour each other. She fingers my pussy thoroughly, she rolls her skates endlessly. I've had my tits sticking out for quite a while and it almost hurts. I invite her to suck me while pushing my fingers into her pussy. The pleasure makes my body contract with each lick. She gets up, takes my hand, and invites me to sit on the cock of Thomas who regained his strength. I ride him, and see that it's been years since his cock has not been this hard. Jade, notices it instinctively, throws me on my stomach, spreads my buttocks as if to invite Thomas to take me from behind. He hesitates, she spits in my anus and hurries to plant a finger there. My body is hot! He finally decides to take me, I feel the head of his cock caressing my ass, and in a moment, in one movement, he sinks it deep. If there was anyone within a radius of ten kilometers, they would certainly have heard my cry. His sex softened, he frees me quickly to take care of Jade. She touches herself. Vibrating with desire, her moans became more and more intense. It's much more exciting than I imagined, hotter. Standing, I rub her pussy fiercely with my legs, and at times, it's my knee knocking on the door, spreading the lips of her swollen and hairy pussy. And finally the dazzling explosion. An almost magical orgasm. Unable to contain the spasms of her lower abdomen, she throws herself on the ground, and gives free rein to orgasmic convulsions, accompanied by a *creampie* like you don't often see. She seems to calm down, but she doesn't seem to have ejected everything. As soon as I introduce a finger, she goes for a new distortion. Thomas masturbates. Ejaculates a drop of cum and lies down. After long minutes of silence, we come closer to lie down all three on the grass, side by side.

We've been in this position for over an hour. We decide to go home. I try to walk but my ass hurts so much. They each take a hand to help me move forward. None of us seem concerned or embarrassed enough about the sextape story to bring up the discussion about it.

We all three stink, and we go upstairs to take a shower.

At the edge of the bathtub, Jade insists on cleaning my anus. Thomas, with a wandering finger, runs through my chest, my stomach, my lower back. He has a hard-on almost vertically and my pussy doesn't seem to interest him: They want to blow my ass. Jade slips away to return with a huge dildo. I'm shaking already! I gently massage the balls of Thomas, back to the wall now. Jade presses me against him. His cock is between my legs, my back against his chest, with one hand he holds my neck, and with the other he presses my breasts, puts my hair to one side to lick my neck. Jade pushes her object gently into my vagina, Thomas manages to penetrate me from behind after several attempts. I try to free myself, but Thomas holds me almost violently. Jade helps him too. They pick up the pace. "Again, damn it," I said repeatedly. He bangs me thoroughly, at a hellish pace. His balls hit me against the ass. I already know that I won't be able to walk straight for a week. I shiver with pleasure. A delicious ecstasy! The body stretched to the extreme. Jade, each time, seems to go deeper into me. They release me at the same time. I almost fall to my knees, but they hold me back. I slip into the bath and say to them: “come on, have fun in my room, on my bed”.

We enjoyed a day like no other. The three of us all have dinner together. Jade tries to bring up the subject of the sextape.

– One day, someone, to whom I am kind enough not to name him, said to me: "Revenge is the memory of evil: forgetting evil is revenge for good." “Launches us Thomas, before continuing, I have nothing so enemy to my health as the “others”, I do not want to explain myself and I do not want to meet anyone.

Alas, what errors and misunderstandings there are in this world! I throw.

Thomas gets up, kisses me tenderly and places an innocent kiss on Jade's temple. Wishing us goodnight, his voice had a melancholy tinge to it.

As soon as he closes the door behind him, Jade places her hand on mine and says in a barely audible voice:

—I have a secret to tell you.

—You already know, when it comes to discretion, I have no equal.

—Look, we need to comb through the whole house. And we'll find an opportunity to do the same with Thomas' residence.

My face crumbles.

– The sextape that is viral now, I already watched it on Léon's laptop, I didn't want to delete it to avoid arousing any suspicion, but the day before yesterday when the video was online, I searched in the laptop, and there were others, I didn't recognize this room, she said pointing to the room, on none of them, but you should be careful.

–Thomas presented me with another version!

– What did he say ?

– That a stranger blackmailed him with this video when he was still in politics, his friends and his enemies all have long arms, and dropping a camera after breaking into a house was very likely, I know a little bit and it was just them, I answer her in such a low voice.

– Listen, before going out with me, Léon was flirting with my brother, I only found out recently when Léon categorically refused to let me invite him to my birthday party, I had doubts, I discussed it with my brother, and he admitted it to me, he also admitted that Léon sent him pictures of me naked with him. I even start to doubt videos of me that would be kept somewhere.

– ...

– The stranger is nothing but your son, she adds, shaking her head.

—Why would he do that? Then, he must have been only 16 years old at the time of the facts!

—...

After an hour of searching, fatigue warns us that we have already searched enough, and reason makes us understand that there is nothing to find. I go up to my room and lie down on my bed. I'm exhausted. Jade will sleep downstairs in the living room.

Thomas would certainly have a heart attack if he discovered that his son stabbed him in the back while handling him in this way. Last year he was dangerously ill; the extreme irritability of his nerves led his doctor to recommend that I keep the slightest negative emotion away from him.

I accompanied him everywhere, I saw him in the pleasures of licentiousness, in the sensualities of intemperance, in the fury of anger, in the failures of fear, in the soft quietudes of laziness, in the agitations of ambition, in the venoms of envy, in the secret violence of fleeting jealousy, but with his son, he is almost a different man. His son is his life, his story, his pride and his raison d'être. Léon's birth gave meaning to his life. He sacrificed himself for him. He gave up several projects just to stay with him and spend more time with him.

I want to call Léon and insult him. But if he lies, how can I prove his lie? I don't even want to bring Jade into this story. If he is capable of such enormity, who would guarantee me that he would not hurt me! He never had any respect for me.

The sound of a car speeding past chills my blood. I don't bode well. The noise is approaching. I get up and run downstairs. Léon, in a rage, runs to grab Jade who is already standing.

"Who the hell told you to come here?" he asks, strangling her against the wall.

I go down the stairs and stumble over my face to the floor. Seeing Thomas arrive, Léon releases Jade.

—How did you know I was here?"

—I tracked your phone because you're a vulgar whore.

— That's all you know how to do, Jade told him with a sly smile after catching her breath before going on, spying on the others, tracking them down, filming them without their knowledge because you're just an asshole who needs attention.

He strangles her again.

"Release her," I ordered, trying to pull him away from her.

He resists.

– Release her son and let's talk, throws Thomas, desperate, certainly came running given his panting breathing.

Léon, in a rage, showing a face of disaster:

– I'm not your son, he replies, releasing Jade, and approaching Thomas, he repeats three times: you're not my father.

Thomas nervously squeezes his hands together, and stares at me questioningly. His kindness keeps him on the slope where his spirit pushes him. He remains pensive. Thomas is constantly in doubt. He doubts simply because he is eager to remain impartial, or else because he is above all concerned with being just and because, finally, he has at heart to express only definitive opinions. But after all, he doesn't give a damn. He loved him, that's really what matters to him. And if that's not enough, I know him well enough to know that in difficult times, his motto is: feed on lies, or be forever miserable, forever sad. Love makes excuses for all the mistakes it causes.

– Do not worry my son, I said to comfort him, when we decided to have a child, we had moved away from everything Thomas and me.

He turns to me, certainly doubting my sincerity, his gaze chilling:

– I've already done the tests, sending our hair to three different clinics, the result is the same, he advances sometimes fixing me sometimes fixing

Thomas, before getting lost in an abundant vocabulary of insults.

Thomas sits down on the floor. I squeeze my chest with my hands as if to keep my heart from tearing it. My silence gives him the greatest anxiety.

—I've lived with this for ten years, he continues with tears in his eyes.

The vibrations of his voice reach my heart. Thomas shudders at the thought of his estrangement.

—They raised you and gave you the best life possible, and even if what you're saying is true, that doesn't excuse the fact that you filmed them and then blackmailed your father, incognito by the way, reproaches Jade, shaking my hand.

Léon burst out laughing. He laughs so hard that tears fall from his eyes, bows and places both hands on his knees. He laughs like crazy.

– Ah the bastard, he said looking at Thomas, you managed to make them swallow that too, turns to us and swings words interspersed with laughter, I'm leaving, ask him for more details, more explanation the next time he tells you something.

A lively astonishment is painted on all faces.

Léon starts the car and drives like crazy, he seemed unwell. The car disappears. It is dreadful to see one's son suffer, and yet it is only then that one really feels how much one loves him. We help Thomas to get up to sit on the couch.

– An explanation is necessary between us, throws me Thomas.

—Indeed, look me in the eye, I told him.

He looks away.

—Look at me," I told him, grabbing his chin.

He stares at me in bewilderment.

—Did you sexually abuse Léon when he was little?

—Never ! he exclaims in a tone that convinces, and goes on, I swear to you, I'm going to tell you everything, it was a mistake to film us, a serious mistake, the video was in my laptop, Léon took it to school because his laptop was not working, and a classmate somehow found it and showed it to the whole class, I didn't want to tell you about it.

– But why ? I exclaimed, reading his face immediately: to save my dignity without compromising my rest, the wisest thing to do was to disappear.

He sighs before answering me:

– I didn't want to worry you, and continues, clasping his hands on the table, I didn't want to see you hurting yourself with shame and pain, the school's director called me, took care of it the same day, he had seized all the students' computers that day to ensure that no copy would fall into the hands of malicious people. I changed schools for Léon, and it broke my heart to put him in such a situation. The day before yesterday, Léon was very angry with you, he published it on the internet, I don't know why he kept it, believe me, he immediately regretted it, he called me, and to protect him, I pretended to be very upset.

—Listen, Jade launches us in a trembling voice, when Léon approached me, I smelled a perfume that I can distinguish among a thousand, it's my brother's, they have certainly gotten back together, I think that Léon was just using me to get them back together, I don't blame him, they are terribly in love with each other, maybe it would be a good idea if you make Léon understand that you be as proud of him as if he married a woman.

—He knows us very well, at least enough for him to realize that we would never have judged his homosexuality, I said, comforting Thomas with my hand on his shoulder.

— Contrary to the image he wants to give of him, he's a boy who lacks self-confidence, she says holding her face in her hands and continues, he's too worried about the rumors of the region.

— I want to meet your brother, I told her.

Little by little, Thomas' face resumed a less sorry expression and said:

- Me too.

After a slight smile, Jade said to me:

– You've already met him, he's the actor you shot the scene with.

–...

–...

– If you watched the film, you would have noticed that he was the headliner, and that I only had a small secondary role, his name is Raphaël.

I never believed that one day I would see my perseverance waver. I feel lukewarm. I don't even have the strength to be as stressed as I should be. I ruminate. There arises in me an apprehension, a slight fear of being disappointed in myself.

– We have to do something, we have to make decisions in order to avoid consequences that we have only too many reasons to fear, Thomas suggests to us, throwing me a sideways glance, and at the same time putting his hand on my knee that I push immediately, but gently.

Jade has a ready answer:

–They have to get married.

Thomas remains pensive for a moment and then resumes suddenly, with that sullen air which is more and more usual to him:

–They have to get married.

5.

Three months have passed. Everything is in order. I gave a few interviews. Léon improvised as an artist's agent for me. He is preparing a new project with a great screenwriter. The film was a commercial success and can now afford a new adventure, with its own means. He made a name for himself. He offered me a role but I don't know, the idea of interrupting my lifestyle and disturbing Thomas is unbearable to me.

He wanted his marriage to Raphaël to be as humble as possible, and they held a small reception in Paris last week. A dozen friends only, and they came to visit us this afternoon.

We're cooking dinner, Jade and I. The morning was so beautiful, everything was so good, so wide awake all around, that the sun seemed to say: "Be happy!" Jade thought she heard it humming poems.

—I was really afraid that he would make the search for his biological father his life's quest, a raison d'être! He's never broached the subject, and he doesn't seem keen on setting the stage for me to talk about it, I tell Jade.

—Thomas, too, told me about it, he was afraid too, she said, before asking me to go get Thomas since dinner is almost ready.

—We're waiting for Léon and Raphaël first, they shouldn't be long.

– I explained to them very well that there is no network in this mountain and that they had to be here at 8 o'clock sharp.

—It's a quarter to.

—They'll be here any minute, they better be here if they don't want to see me upset, she said before breaking into childish laughter.

Thomas arrives with two bottles of champagne. He then places a carnal kiss on Jade's lips before doing the same with me, while scanning the door. Jade throws me a knowing look mingled with a slight smile before offering a light spanking to

Thomas, a little embarrassed. We discussed it; when Léon and Raphaël are around, we behave as if we were simple friends even if they know everything. Because they are aware of everything, and since they are happy for us, we prefer to return the favor by sparing them a few details.

They arrive. Raphaël is holding a branch on which three roses bloom. He cuts it in half, gives me one and offers the other to Jade. He is filled with an indefinable charm. Léon too. They are beautiful. They are more beautiful together. Raphaël is both a little effeminate but quite virile. What is striking about him, at first sight, is this slowness of movement, this nonchalance of pose, this softness of pace. His muscles seem to disdain all effort and instinctively seek rest, even if he is rather well built.

We dine together all six. Thomas, Léon, Jade, Raphaël and me. Pleasure is the sixth. The kitchen overlooks the garden. It's raining, timidly. A light, fragrant breeze gently stirs the plants in my vegetable garden and caresses my pretty hen with frightened shivers. Raphaël takes out his smartphone and shows us the child they want to adopt. We congratulate them.

—Léon blames himself for not having written to you often enough in recent weeks, but you should excuse him, his head was so little to him and each time he wanted to write to you, he had trouble putting two ideas together, Raphaël tells us.

—It doesn't matter," Thomas and I shouted at the same time.

—Otherwise, you feel better father-in-law? The last time you looked a bit tired to me, Raphaël resumes.

—The king is not my cousin ! he answers. That's an old saying meaning joy, you know it?

—And you're in a good position to use the expression," Jade said, having rubbed shoulders with thc upper echelons.

—Believe me, in this sphere, immorality reigns everywhere, around the throne, at the foot of the throne, on the throne, far from the throne, everywhere. The ancients naively believed that if kings ceased to exist, there would be no more wars, no more glory in being a noble warrior, the republican presidents then invented several types of warriors who make their crimes forgotten by more bigger crimes.

We make such a pout that he stops in the middle of his philosophical quip.

The air sparkles, such is the ardor of the hour. All become more and more necessary to me. The last time when they were here, Raphaël gave me a USB key and a letter of apology, signed Raphaël and Léon. It contains all the videos and the USB is the last medium containing them. I forgave them both. Raphaël insisted on explaining that it was he who prompted Léon to publish the video, justifying this by an unconditional love for him, and by a moment of exasperation. And he spoke with a shudder which it was impossible for him to conceal. I understand them. It always goes that way. Young people who have not yet experienced a world where selfishness stifles the esteem of others, and should be tempered when one becomes aware of it because it strangles proud aspirations, discolors beautiful dreams, dries up the heart, kills devotion and uncalculated enthusiasm for holy causes. They believe, they love, they have the very enviable happiness of being able to admire, and they admire. They admire each other. They're happy. Happy to be together, happy to breathe the same air. I caught them this morning throwing pillows at each other. Raphaël is a happy man: pinched mouth, brown mustache, smooth and slightly turned up, he finds an infinite charm in living, and a coquettish smile always puckers his lips .

With Jade, and despite our frankness, we sometimes speak in riddles. We must not imagine the woman, we must take her as she is. If we neglect her and everything crumbles, if we seize her and everything remains. There is no nobler, more lively, more moving poetry than her story and mine. We walked together, unevenly, each to their own destiny, and we ended up joining in a common triumph.

Something in me seems to be certain of it: she wants to convert me. She never talks to me about it, but I sense she would be delighted to see me choose a god and worship him sincerely, even in the distant future. Like a belated act of faith, a magical moment that brings the lost sheep back to the fold and ensures its salvation. Believer! I who have always seen with a favorable eye those who ruin religion from the base, because deep down, I have never appreciated the way in which God uses men to convert peoples.

Months and years pass like a dream. But life can surprise at any time. Before two months, Thomas led a life of oysters, today, he discovers a new youth. And soon he will be a grandfather.

My biggest regret is not having understood Léon, not having understood that the most beautiful half of the human race is not necessarily a woman. From adolescence, I guessed the girls burned in secret for Léon. I was having fun sketching the perfect woman for him, and neglecting how he felt. Maybe it's because my early youth was tormented. Already at the end of adolescence, unhappy, constantly occupied with voluptuous thoughts, I fled society, and, in solitude, I abandoned myself to the disorder of my passion, satisfying, by lascivious touches, the immoderate need that dominated. And, in the midst of all this, my imagination, with its seductive illusions, shimmered with a deceptive brilliance all the things of love. Before discovering with

Thomas, later, a licentiousness superior to its reputation. And there had been no lack of sense or virtue. I will never forgive myself for my awkwardness, but I have no time to blame myself any longer. I prefer to think about my past with Thomas. We had sex with Arab diplomats in a hammam in Jordan. With strangers at a nudist beach in Miami. In Berlin, a swingers' club introduced us to all kinds of extravagance. Several hotels in Milan still remember my cries. In Thailand, Thomas loved seeing a stranger fuck me in the pool, which was crowded with people. Sometimes we would go to a concert, and the first to make advances to me, Thomas encouraged him to take me in the middle of a concert, to the rhythm of the music and the fires. We fucked in an elevator, behind a truck, in a mansion and in a hut in Africa. In an abandoned village in Siberia and in the most prestigious area of London. In the rain, on the snow, and in the middle of the desert, under a stifling sun, where the void began, not far from a few lost tribes, wandering in the sands, and in narrow oases. I have seen the world, and wherever woman is considered, man is free and virtuous. I gave pleasure to a Goncourt prize, a Nobel prize and an illiterate peasant who began to love light and color, as his fathers loved the earth. I received in me the seed of Asians, blacks and Arabs, and lots of other races. Worshipers of all religions; retailers of the same wholesaler, who make their followers believe that the pleasures of the world are a trap, atheists and irreligious. Dwarves and giants. Young and old. Thomas took me to see dreamers and men who have no other horizons than the obligations of a modest existence. He has invited into our bed men who are both humble and realistic, and men who, as soon as they decipher a few pages of the book of life, believe themselves to be of a superior essence. Women too, lots of women. Some were lucid, others naive, and did not know before approaching us that there were other ways of living in this world. Some seemed to have known light only in the dubious state of twilight, or in the violent state of brilliance. Some allowed me to discover myself a little more. Some worried about their image, and were afraid of losing votes if their homosexuality were to make headlines. But we were discreet, like a confessor. People criticize some platforms for promoting gays and lesbians too much. I have a better, simpler idea. For Netflix to stop making such productions, the LGBTQ+ cause would have to be so well established in the order that nothing would be able to make it fall from it. That people face the facts, which is inevitable, we must admit it now. Because love always ends up imposing itself, whatever detours we take to delay its triumph. Unfortunately, that's not likely to happen any time soon. Everywhere the people have against them traditions of which they themselves are sometimes the first dupe or the complacent naive.

We became almost full time nudists, Thomas, Jade and me. We love spending a lot of naked time outside. Sometimes goats surprise us, a rare peasant or a curious bird. I've always dreamed of this. I have a great desire to go away, alone, to wander through the countryside: the vanished dream would soon be reborn, I'm sure. But don't I have tomorrow, and weeks?

– We have news to tell you, Jade launches to break a silence that has lasted too long, and continues by joining her hand on Thomas's on the table and placing the other on my shoulder, I'm expecting a child!

Raphaël jumps for joy and applauds like a child. Léon congratulates

Thomas and kisses Jade, and without really knowing what he is saying, he says it well, with joy. Raphaël gets up from his chair and kisses my temple, and says:

—We are very happy, and we would like to see you as happy as we are."

– I almost forgot, says Léon, who seemed to avoid speaking, and leaves to come back then with a canvas behind his back, advancing towards me, mum, he says, a security guard told me that you stayed a long time contemplating this painting, I even contacted the artist for more explanations, and he was categorical, the sun rises there.

He sent me a note too. An ancient popular verse, and promised me a painting dedicated to me:

Devotees preach night and day

Against the pleasures of love.

But no matter how much they say, we laugh at it.

If this sin were punished,

It would be necessary, says a debauchee,

Fill the paradise with straw.

The moon in the sky looks drunk. It reminds me of the first poem I learned by heart for a play:

I would have let the sea breeze come into my huge halls;

I would have touched my organs and sung my part

To the chorale of the Ocean, Solitude and Ennui.

I would have dreamed, far from everything, far from men and far perhaps from my life,

Harmonious, eyes wandering on the eternal wave, which always swells and always falls,

Or, on calm winter evenings, staring into the embers and ashes of the hearth in the apse,

I would have dreamed without brake without memory and without limit, at the altar of my passions.

END

Contact :

annamaillardlamy@gmail.com

Twitter: @AnnaMaillardLam

www.ingramcontent.com/pod-product-compliance
Lightning Source LLC
LaVergne TN
LVHW010611160826
845677LV00013B/3366

* 9 7 9 8 3 6 6 6 2 4 5 6 5 *